DEDICATION

This book is dedicated to all the children of the world and their handfuls of hope. There is always someone looking out for you all! Continue to dream, to believe and to hope!

To Tracy and Inez, the most amazing human beings whose hearts are bigger than one can imagine. Your compassion, benevolence and dedication ensured that many households had food on their tables during these unfamiliar and uncertain times.

A HANDFUL OF HOPE

Copyright © 2022
Renata Ramoino & Sarah-Leigh Wills

Paperback ISBN: 978-1-7397194-0-1

Illustration and design by Happydesigner
www.happydesigner.co.uk

A HANDFUL OF HOPE

Inspired by true events

Renata Ramoino

Illustrated by Sarah-Leigh Wills

A LITTLE WHITE BOX

Rumi's eyes fluttered open. The dawn chorus sounded like a magical melody. She wriggled and stretched in the warmth of her cosy bed. Rubbing the sleep from her eyes, Rumi peeped through the curtain. The sun had painted the sky a streaky strawberry sherbet, and for a little while, Rumi admired the view. Her skin tingled and her face lit up just thinking about today. It also happened to be a Friday.

As quiet as a needle pulling thread, Rumi snuck out of her bedroom so as not to wake her baby brother, who was still soundly asleep with his tiny thumb in his mouth. He looked adorable, she thought.

The house was still, unmoving. She tiptoed down the hallway and slipped through the ajar bathroom door. "Happy birthday to me, happy birthday to me..." Rumi sang softly while washing her hands. The song took on a new meaning. Everyone sang it at school and it gradually became the soundtrack to the children's daily lives. Today was a special occasion, so she didn't mind singing it again, and for even longer this time. She wished her best friends, Charlie and Gigi, could celebrate her birthday with her. Tears like silvery droplets of morning dew fell from her eyes when she realised no one was coming.

Rumi overheard her mum on the phone the other day, saying that they would be penniless now. She had no idea what the word meant, but deep down she knew that it had something to do with her mum losing her job. The following day, her mummy came home very upset and did not bring Rumi's favourite doughnut, as she usually did.

She looked in the mirror and saw tiny freckles scattered across her nose like frisky dots on her favourite dress. Wisps of hair cradled her wet face. Gently, she brushed them away. What she really wished for was for her mum to be happy and for a birthday cake. She craved a rainbow unicorn cake with lashings of white, buttery icing and chocolate inside; the kind that oozes with moisture and becomes irresistibly stuck to your fingers. But would she get one? Her eight-year-old heart began to pound.

"Happy birthday, darling," said her mum while giving her a peck on her cheek. She smelled of freshly brewed coffee and vanilla waffles which lifted Rumi's spirits. "Would you like to see your present?"

"Yes, please."

On the kitchen table, lay a box. Rumi's hopes soared. Inside, hidden under many layers of thin paper, was a pink unicorn with a white horn. Rumi gasped.

"Sorry, my dear, that's all I could get you," her mum said, kissing her daughter once again.

"Thank you mummy, it's beautiful. I will cherish it." She spent the day playing with her new toy, trying to ignore lingering thoughts of the cake.

A squeal of wheels outside jolted her. Rumi leapt to the window. Every Friday, her teacher, Mrs Tullah, came to her house to deliver food. Fireworks exploded in Rumi's chest every time she saw her. Today was no different.

Seeing Mrs Tullah reminded her of school, her friends and all the fun she had been missing. She dashed to the door and swung it open.

"Hello Mrs Tullah. It's great to see you. We've been waiting for you!"

"I am delighted to see you too, Rumi," her teacher said, giving her a huge air hug. "I hope you are doing well and staying safe." She placed two heavy bags of food at the door. Rumi peeked inside. She noticed some apples, a packet of honey flakes, a carton of milk and a little white box. The teacher followed Rumi's gaze and said, with an encouraging smile, "Open it Rumi, this one is especially for you."

Nestled in the box, was a freshly baked chocolate cupcake topped with lashings of white icing and a rainbow unicorn. Rumi stared. A teasing smell tickled her nostrils and she felt her freckles bounce. With a trembling finger, she eagerly scooped a mound of icing, closed her eyes and indulged. She savoured every morsel of it.

"I hope you like it," Mrs Tullah chuckled. "There is also a colouring book and a pencil set.

"How —" she cleared her throat. "How did you know, Miss?" Rumi was dizzy with joy; her feet barely touched the ground.

"I know my pupils really well," she winked. "Happy birthday, my lovely, and enjoy the cake."

And with that, her teacher was gone. Until next Friday...

A BIG BROWN ENVELOPE

It was a Tuesday and Charlie was looking forward to Mrs Tullah's new assignment. He had been waiting for another chapter of his new favourite book to be read.

Since online learning started, Charlie has always completed every task. His mummy was helping and guiding him, but he knew he had to work hard in order to write those ps, ys and qs properly. In her videos, Mrs Tullah constantly prompted them: "Remember children, the long letters are long and their bellies sit on the line." Despite Charlie's best efforts, the cheeky letters wouldn't listen. At least not all of them.

He was all alone today. His mum was distraught after a stranger in the supermarket yelled at her, "Go back to your country – you're not welcome here!" Charlie didn't understand what the people meant by saying that. Back at home, she shut herself in the bedroom and did not come out for a very long time. His dad's attempts to console her were fruitless. Charlie was confused and unable to make sense of the events unfolding around him.

The moment he clicked on the link, a familiar face popped up on his computer screen. He listened to his teacher read and tried to concentrate when answering the questions, but his mind was like a lost puppy wandering around.

Charlie had made two mistakes, but he was nonetheless pleased with himself. "We learn from our mistakes," he recalled Mrs Tullah telling them at school. Every time his teacher read another chapter, she taught them a new word. Perseverance was the word of the day. It was a tricky one to pronounce and it took Charlie several attempts before he got it right. He liked the meaning of the word; 'to keep trying to achieve something even

though it is challenging.' So he would persevere and correctly write those ps and qs.

Charlie was about to begin his Science lesson when, out of the blue, the doorbell rang. His mum emerged from the bedroom, wiping her tears away and forcing a smile.

"Who could that be?" she wondered, glancing around the room warily. They were not expecting anyone.

"Hello Charlie. How are you today?" A friendly voice greeted him. At the door, wearing a huge smile on her face, stood Mrs Tullah. A smidgeon of her perfume drifted across the air, evoking fond memories.

Charlie's jaw dropped. He just saw his teacher on the computer screen teaching a new word and now she was standing outside his front door! Thunderstruck, he couldn't utter a word.

"I'm here to deliver your certificate, which you earned for your efficient work, Charlie," she explained.

Puzzled, Charlie put his hand over his mouth. He didn't believe certificates awarded online were for real. It was out of this world to see his teacher standing in front of him. He'd missed her, his friends, and – interestingly enough – even school lunches. It was his friend Rumi's birthday the other day, but he couldn't go; none of them could...

Seeing Mrs Tullah gave him a glimmer of hope that normality would return soon.

Grinning like a tabby kitten, Charlie took the brown envelope his teacher had handed him. Inside, there was a certificate (which smelled like jelly beans), a whiteboard, some markers and a book about dragons. Charlie was a dragon aficionado.

"Hooray! This is so cool!" he shrieked, as his mum snapped a photo of him clutching everything he had found in the brown envelope.

As she walked away, Mrs Tullah heard Charlie's words. She experienced a strange sense of fulfilment that the words could not describe. She'd delivered forty-two brown envelopes so far and she'd gladly double or triple this number just to see her pupils' thrilled faces again. It was at times like these when she loved her job the most.

A PAPER BAG

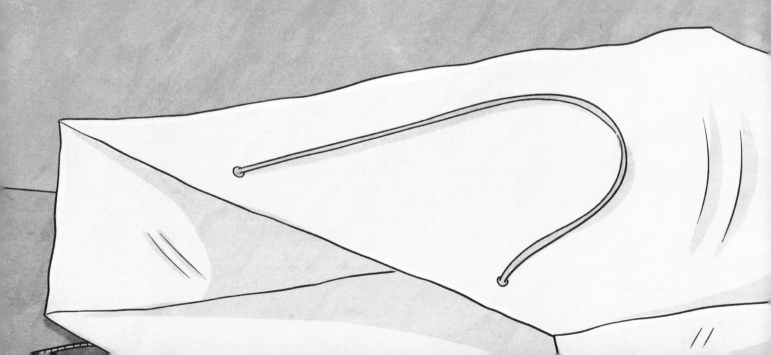

Rain pelted against the kitchen window. Grey pillows of clouds hung like massive chandeliers over the city. Even though the sky was raging today, it didn't seem to bother Gigi in the least. She was elated.

"Mrs Tullah is coming today. Mrs Tullah is on her way," Gigi sang throughout the morning. She skipped and clapped her hands when she found out that her beloved teacher would be arriving soon.

"Eat some breakfast, Gigi," her father urged as he pushed a bowl of cereal towards her.

"I'm not hungry, daddy."

"Is your tummy full of excitement?" asked her mum.

"I wish Rumi and Charlie could come too so we could play Tag." A tiny pang gripped Gigi's heart. "When could they come?"

Her dad squirmed in his seat, staring out of the window, unable to meet his daughter's eyes. "I don't know, my dear. I don't know anything anymore," he sighed.

"It's time to do your lessons, Gigi!" Her mum called.

Every day, she sat at the computer screen, transfixed, and listened to her teacher. It felt surreal, yet also strangely familiar. On a few occasions, Gigi and her mum floundered, their visions blurred while watching Mrs Tullah. They'd pause the videos and stare at her amicable face, as if seeking answers. The family hadn't left the house in a long time and they felt confined within its walls.

Today was an extraordinary day. Gigi had prepared for it with great care. She asked her mum to wash her school uniform using the new fabric conditioner that the Tesco man had delivered a week ago. It had the scent of outdoor freshness with a tinge of lemon in it. Once the outfit was perfectly ironed, everything was in order. Enthusiastically, Gigi put on the uniform, knotted her favourite ribbons in her hair and slipped into her school shoes. She swirled and twirled like Angelina Ballerina in Miss Lilly's ballet class.

Stacked into towering heaps, the books formed a fortress in Gigi's room. Books surrounded her, books gawked at her, books conversed with her. She'd read each and every one of them at least twice.

Unfortunately, the library was closed and she had a long list of new titles she hoped to read. Perhaps one day...

When Mrs Tullah called to check on things, Gigi shared her dream with the teacher.

"Mrs Tullah, I finished reading all of my books. Could I please have some new?"

"Of course, Gigi. Do you have a list of the books you wish for?"
"Yes, Miss!" she exclaimed.

The following day, while marking children's work on line, Mrs Tullah received a long list and messaged Gigi back, promising to visit soon.

Today was the day. Swaying their legs side to side, Gigi and her big sister sat on the bed lost in their thoughts. Gigi's mind was like a hurricane sweeping across the globe. One minute, she was at school learning about the Great Fire of London. The next, she found herself roaming through the pitch black forest where Hansel and Gretel had been abandoned by their stepmother. Yet another…

A knock on the door startled them. Faster than thought, Gigi jumped off the bed and darted to the door. Her dad and sister could hardly keep up. She flung it open and there, smiling as always, stood Mrs Tullah. The sun had decided to make an appearance and wrapped them both in its snuggly embrace. The air was crisp and tasted delicious after the rain.

Greedily, Gigi inhaled its freshness again and again. It felt so good to be outside. They stood and gazed at each other for what seemed like eternity. Mrs Tullah told her about the school and the children who were allowed to attend. In return, Gigi chatted about her favourite online learning and the books she'd read. Gigi talked and talked, and her teacher listened with a nod and a grin to accompany her interest. They both felt as if nothing had changed, that the world remained the same, just having the worst dream ever.

"Here are some books for you and your sister to read," Mrs Tullah said as she handed Gigi a large paper bag. The expressions on the girls' faces were priceless and it made the teacher giggle. In astonishment, the sisters flicked through the storybooks, unable to decide which they liked more.

"Thank you, thank you, thank you," whispered Gigi's sister.

"This is the best day ever!" Bliss tugged at the corners of Gigi's lips as if invisible fairies were playing tug-of-war.

Without a shadow of a doubt, this was one of the best days in Mrs Tullah's life too.

September finally arrived. Schools reopened their doors and eagerly greeted their students. Rumi was late as it took a long time to find her school shoes. Cosily tucked away, they were at the farthest end of the shoe rack, as if playing hide and seek. She walked to her classroom and stood against the outside wall. Cautiously, Rumi glanced around. Her dreamy eyes searched for familiar faces and places; everything looked the same as before... kind of.

"Hello, Rumi." She turned around and saw Mrs Tullah standing right behind her. Her eyes glimmered in the sunlight.

"Hello Mrs Tullah, lovely to see you," she said. "I was looking forward to this day and here we are again." A dimpled smile sprang on Rumi's face.

"Yes, here we are. Shall we go inside?"

Rumi followed her teacher and saw Charlie and Gigi waving at her. The children bowed and curtsied to one another as these were the new ways of greeting. Their little faces were worried and excited at the same time. They were back where they belonged.

A short moment later, Mrs Tullah asked the children to sit on the carpet in a circle. She placed a rainbow-coloured jar in the middle and gave each child a post-it note.

"That's like a rainbow in my window!" squeaked the girl wearing a navy headscarf.

Mrs Tullah nodded and asked, "How are you all feeling today?"

Everyone looked at their teacher, uncertainty etched on their faces.

"I'm really nervous," said Charlie, "but I'm also happy to see my friends."

"I'm very shy because I don't know anyone," whispered the boy with thick-rimmed glasses.

"Can we go outside to play please?" asked Gigi, while fiddling with the hem of her skirt. A faint sigh escaped her body as she gazed at the playground.

Mrs Tullah asked the children to write their feelings and emotions on the note, fold it and drop inside the rainbow jar. She kindly explained that all their worries would go away if they shared them.

"It is okay not to be okay," she said and rewarded her pupils with a comforting smile.

Silence descended. But it was short-lived. The children looked at each other, their searching eyes darting back and forth. Soon, the classroom came to life, and cheerful voices echoed around the room.

Rumi approached Gigi, "Shall we go play Tag? Charlie and others are coming too." Everyone raced out into the world that was so dear and close to their hearts. The world that every child should be able to enjoy without any fear or restriction.

Mrs Tullah leaned against the door and followed her pupils with a fond gaze. A siren's piercing cry in the distance broke the silence. She flinched. But as soon as it began, it came to an end. Deep in her heart, she knew that everything would be okay. Sooner or later, all will be fine. A different sort of fine – with a handful of hope.

ABOUT THE AUTHOR

Renata is a primary school teacher who adores reading and learning something new every day. She is passionate about creative writing and provides a language-rich classroom for her pupils in order to stimulate their imagination.

She is an avid globetrotter, always looking forward to escaping somewhere new.

ACKNOWLEDGMENTS

I would like to thank my wonderfully patient husband, who believes in me, always encourages me and motivates me to achieve my dreams.

Huge thanks to my dear friend Shayeemah for her valuable advice and assistance in the book's editing process.

Printed in Great Britain
by Amazon

81404601R00025